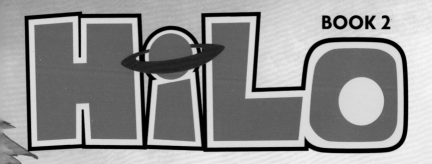

BOOK 2

SAVING THE WHOLE WIDE WORLD

BY **JUDD WINICK**

COLOUR BY GUY MAJOR

KU-317-761

PUFFIN

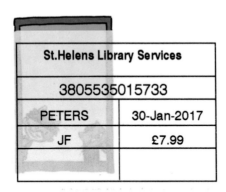

PUFFIN BOOKS

UK | USA | Canada | Ireland | Australia | India | New Zealand | South Africa

Puffin Books is part of the Penguin Random House group of companies whose addresses can be found at global.penguinrandomhouse.com.

www.penguin.co.uk   www.puffin.co.uk   www.ladybird.co.uk

First published in the United States of America by Random House Children's Books, a division of Random House LLC, 2016
Published in Great Britain by Puffin Books 2017

001

Book design by John Sazaklis

Printed in China

A CIP catalogue record for this book is available from the British Library

ISBN: 978-0-141-37690-5

All correspondence to:
Puffin Books
Penguin Random House Children's
80 Strand, London WC2R 0RL

MIX
Paper from
responsible sources
FSC® C018179

Penguin Random House is committed to a sustainable future for our business, our readers and our planet. This book is made from Forest Stewardship Council® certified paper.

HERE'S WHAT PEOPLE ARE SAYING ABOUT

"Fast paced, **FURIOUSLY FUNNY,** and will have kids waiting on the edge of their seats for more."
—Jeffrey Brown, JEDI ACADEMY

"BETTER THAN THE BEST!"
—Matteo H-G, age 9

"UNIVERSALLY APPEALING . . . A wholeheartedly **WEIRD** and **WONDERFUL** tale of friendship, acceptance, and robots."
—*Kirkus Reviews*

"HILO **IS MY NEW FAVORITE BOOK. YOU'LL LOVE IT."**
—Aiden B, age 8

"**I** WAIT NEX
—E

"A MUST-HAVE."
—*School Library Journal*

"*Hilo* is delightful, **SILLY,** tender, and most importantly: **FUNNY.**"
—Jeff Smith, author of the BONE series

"GINA IS SO AWESOME. She's not afraid of anything and really cares about her friend! Mum, can I have my book back?!"
—Kyla G, age 10

"A PERFECT BOOK for any kid who ever needed a friend and then had one with superpowers fall from space." —Seth Meyers, actor and comedian

"More **GIANT ROBOTIC ANTS . . .** than in the complete works of Jane Austen."
—Neil Gaiman, CORALINE

For Pam

CHAPTER

1

A LITTLE WEIRD

I'LL TRY TO EXPLAIN, BUT IT WAS A LITTLE WEIRD.

MY NAME IS **DANIEL JACKSON LIM**, BUT EVERYONE CALLS ME **D.J.** AND I WASN'T GOOD AT ANYTHING.

THEN A BOY FELL FROM THE SKY.

BOOM

BUT HE **WASN'T** A BOY.

HE WAS A **ROBOT**. HE CAME FROM ANOTHER **DIMENSION**.

HIS NAME WAS **HILO**.

AAAH!

HE WAS AWESOME.

HE LIKED TO BURP A LOT. HE WAS REALLY LOUD.

OUTSTANDING!

AND HE WAS MY FRIEND.

HE STOPPED A BUNCH OF EVIL ROBOTS FROM DESTROYING EARTH.

IT WAS HARD, BUT HIS JOB ON HIS PLANET IS STOPPING BAD ROBOTS. SO HE'S PRETTY GOOD AT IT.

THEN HE WAS GONE.

AT LEAST I THOUGHT HE WAS GONE. **NOW** HE'S BACK. MOSTLY BACK.

WHAT IS THAT?

MY TOE.

EW.

YEAH, HE'S TALKING THROUGH HIS TOE. LIKE I SAID, IT'S A LITTLE WEIRD.

YOU SEE IT?

YES.

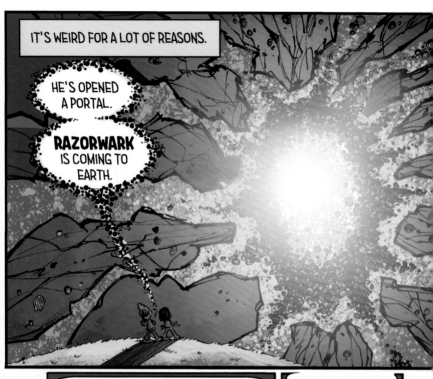

IT'S WEIRD FOR A LOT OF REASONS.

HE'S OPENED A PORTAL.

RAZORWARK IS COMING TO EARTH.

RAZORWARK? THE GIANT KILLER ROBOT THAT'S TRYING TO WIPE OUT HUMANITY ON **YOUR** PLANET IS COMING TO EARTH?!

YEAH. SO, **THAT'S** NOT GREAT.

NO. NOT GREAT.

WHERE ARE YOU?!

I THINK IN A VOID.

VOID?! WHAT'S A VOID?!

NOTHING! IT'S THIS HUUUUGE EMPTY NOTHING PLACE BETWEEN DIMENSIONS! JUST LOTSA PORTALS. SPACE JUNK. SMELLS LIKE A GORILLA'S ARMPIT.

OH, AND RAZORWARK IS HERE.

YOU'RE FIGHTING RAZORWARK?!

NOT SO MUCH FIGHTING AS RUNNING LIKE CRAZY. HE FOLLOWED ME IN HERE -- **WHOA!!**

WHAT?!

JUST GOT HURLED INTO A NEW SPOT. SMELLS LIKE ELEPHANT BUTT.

YIKES!

WHAT?!

NOTHING! WELL ... A LOT ACTUALLY.

HANG ON! HEADS UP! GRAB THIS THING COMING OUT OF THE PORTAL!

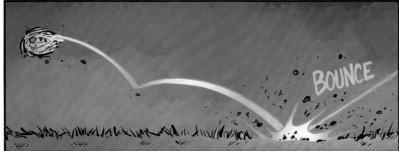

7

SO THE REST OF ME CAN GET THROUGH.

OKAY, FELLAS! PLAYTIME'S OVER! EVERYBODY OUT OF THE POOL!

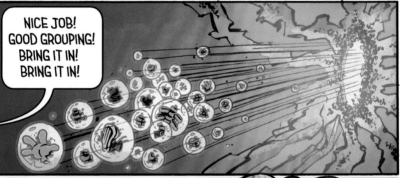

NICE JOB! GOOD GROUPING! BRING IT IN! BRING IT IN!

PLEP PLEP

NICE.

GOOD!

A LITTLE TO THE LEFT!

PLEP PLEP PLEP PLEP

POP

YEAH!

I DIG IT WHEN ALL THE PIECES FIT!

HOW DO I LOOK? TALLER? I WAS HOPING FOR TALLER.

HILO! SOMETHING'S HAPPENING!

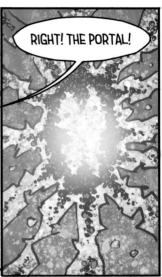

RIGHT! THE PORTAL!

Y'SEE, I LURED RAZORWARK INTO THIS LIMBO.

LURED. ISN'T IT A GREAT WORD? **LURED :** *VERB, PAST TENSE.* TO TEMPT A PERSON OR ANIMAL TO DO SOMETHING OR GO SOMEWHERE. I --

HILO!

YES! RIGHT! I LURED HIM INTO THE VOID AND NOW HE'S STUCK THERE! WE JUST HAVE TO WAIT FOR THE PORTAL TO EXPLODE AND SEAL HIM IN.

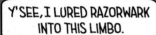

11

BhbOP

AND **THAT**, MY FRIENDS, IS HOW YOU CLOSE A PORTAL!

BOOM!

SO, RAZORWARK IS TRAPPED IN THAT VOID?

YEP! STUCK AND STUCK **GOOD.** AND HE IS **NOT** GONNA BE HAPPY ABOUT THAT.

WHAT ABOUT YOU? WILL YOU STAY HERE ON EARTH?

I GUESS I WILL. I CAN'T OPEN A PORTAL BACK TO MY WORLD, SO I CAN'T LEAVE.

IS IT OKAY IF I STAY?

DEEP

COOM

SPLORCH

PLECK

PLECK

HOP

HOP

SPROUT

SPROUT

SPROUT

CHAPTER 2

KNOCK KNOCK

KNOCK KNOCK!

WHO'S THERE?

INTERRUPTING COW.

INTERRUPTING COW WH--

MOO!

HA HA HA HA HA HA HA HA!

THAT'S GOOD.

GLAD YOU LIKE IT. HE'S GOING TO TELL YOU IT AGAIN.

KNOCK KNOCK!

SCHOOL IS NOT SO FUN, THOUGH ...

YOU'RE SUCH A DWEEB, LIM.

VANDERBILT ELEMENTA

TEAM CAPTAIN OF THE DWEEB TEAM.

MORE LIKE KING OF THE DWEEBS.

WHATEVER. CAN I GO NOW?

NAH, HE'S NOT A DWEEB. HE'S MORE LIKE A **BUG.** YOU DON'T EVEN KNOW HE'S THERE.

YEAH! UNTIL HE CREEPS OUT IN FRONT OF YOU AND THAT'S WHEN HE GETS STEPPED ON!

HA HA HA HA HA HA HA

WHAT'S FUNNY? DID D.J. TELL YOU THAT KNOCK KNOCK JOKE?

KNOCK KNOCK JOKE? WHAT ARE YOU? FOUR YEARS OLD?

NO, WE DON'T KNOW HOW OLD I AM.

HILO...

BUT I HAVE THE **APPEARANCE** OF A TEN-YEAR-OLD. KIND OF LIKE YOU, JASON.

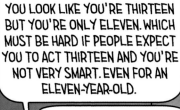

YOU LOOK LIKE YOU'RE THIRTEEN BUT YOU'RE ONLY ELEVEN. WHICH MUST BE HARD IF PEOPLE EXPECT YOU TO ACT THIRTEEN AND YOU'RE NOT VERY SMART. EVEN FOR AN ELEVEN-YEAR-OLD.

YOU CALLING ME STUPID?

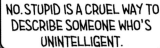

NO. STUPID IS A CRUEL WAY TO DESCRIBE SOMEONE WHO'S UNINTELLIGENT.

BUT ITS USAGE IS APPLICABLE.

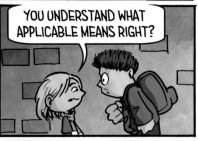

YOU UNDERSTAND WHAT APPLICABLE MEANS RIGHT?

OH NO.

"OH NO"? WHAT? YOU GONNA HIT ME, DORK?

NO. NOT ME.

22

23

HE'S MY FRIEND. I DON'T LET PEOPLE HURT MY FRIENDS.

THAT'S WHAT I ALWAYS SAY!

GINA!

HEY, CONNIE. HEY, BONNIE.

YOU'RE GOING TO BE LATE FOR CHEERLEADING PRACTICE.

AGAIN!

I'LL BE THERE.

MOM SAID IF YOU'RE LATE FOR ANOTHER PRACTICE, SHE'S GOING TO MAKE YOU QUIT ONE OF YOUR NERD CLUBS.

I'LL BE THERE.

YEAH. OR YOU GOTTA QUIT THE MATH BOOK TEAM. OR THE TELESCOPE SOCIETY. UCK. WHATEVER.

I'LL BE THERE.

YOU **BETTER** BE.

AND YOUR HAIR **STILL** LOOKS WEIRD AND FUNNY.

FUNNY?! YOU WANT TO HEAR SOMETHING FUNNY?

TELL THAT KNOCK KNOCK JOKE AGAIN AND I WILL **BEAT** YOU!

SO YOU **DON'T** WANT TO HEAR IT?!

MY SISTERS ARE BEING MEAN TO HILO. YOU WANT TO PUNCH THEM?

THEY'D KILL ME.

TOTALLY WOULD KILL YOU.

MEANWHILE ...

BERKE BOWL

25

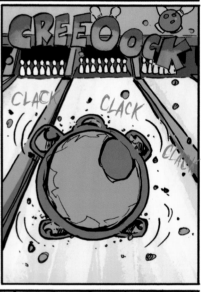

HEY. YOU GUYS HEAR THAT?

HEAR WHAT?

YOU GETTING ONE OF YOUR FEELINGS? LIKE WHEN A **RANT** ROBOT IS COMING?

NO. I MEAN **HEAR.** BUT IT'S REALLY FAR AWAY.

HOLY MACKEREL! I MIGHT HAVE SUPER-DUPER HEARING. LIKE **DOGS!** YOU FELLAS HEAR SOMETHING?

WHAT DOES IT SOUND LIKE, HILO?

LIKE ... METAL?

WHOA!

YEAH.

LOOK AT **THAT!**

YEAH.

I THINK THAT'S THE METAL YOU'RE HEARING.

27

28

BOWLING BALLS!! HE'S CHUCKING BOWLING BALLS!!

B.O.I.D.! B.O.I.D.! B.O.I.D.!
BEING OF INDETERMINATE DESIGNATION!
DESTROY! DESTROY! DESTROY!

D.J.?

YEAH?

THIS IS WHEN I NEED TO PUSH BACK.

34

POOF

TUNK

TZZZZZZZZ

BEEEOoooooP

HE SHORT-CIRCUITED?

YEAH. I COULD TELL HIS OUTER SHELL WASN'T MADE TO GET WET.

AND I DIDN'T WANT TO HURT HIM. NO MORE HURTING ROBOTS.

SINCE WHEN?

SINCE NOW.

I THOUGHT YOUR JOB BACK ON YOUR WORLD WAS TO STOP BAD ROBOTS?

IT WAS! I DID! AND I'LL KEEP DOING THAT. BUT I'M NOT GOING TO WRECK THEM ANYMORE.

Pat

WHAT IF ROBOTS ARE HURTING PEOPLE?

GINA.

WHAT IF ROBOTS ARE HURTING **PEOPLE?**

I CAN STOP BAD MACHINES WITHOUT DESTROYING THEM.

NOBODY GETS HURT. NOT ROBOTS. NOT PEOPLE.

NO ONE.

37

CHAPTER

HILO'S HOUSE

LOOK! D.J.'S MOM AND SISTER ARE HERE.

HILO! QUICK, HIDE THE --

GOT IT.

SPLORCH

HEY, MOM!

HEY, MRS. LIM!

OH! HI!

HI, D.J.! HI, GINA!

HEY, HILO.

HEY, LISA!

I WAS JUST PICKING UP LISA FROM HER PIANO LESSON AT MR. KENNEDY'S. WHAT ARE YOU THREE UP TO?

SOLVING A MYSTERY.

NOTHING!

NOTHING! WE ARE NOT DOING ANYTHING!

WHAT'S THE MYSTERY, HILO?

YOU DON'T WANT ME TO TELL. YOU ALWAYS LIKE FIGURING STUFF OUT.

WELL, WHY DON'T THE TWO OF YOU JOIN US FOR DINNER? HILO, MAYBE YOU COULD INVITE YOUR UNCLE TROUT?

HE WON'T COME.

NO. HE WON'T.

HELLO THERE!

HOW ARE YOU?!

I'M FINE, TROUT! I WAS JUST ASKING THE KIDS IF YOU'D LIKE TO JOIN US FOR DINNER!

I'D LOVE TO! BUT I'VE GOT PILES TO DO HERE! AND I'M GETTING READY TO BARBECUE!

TOLD YOU.

MAYBE ANOTHER TIME!

YES! WE COULD GO FOR A SWIM!

41

42

43

HILO THROWS UP IF HE EATS MEAT, CHICKEN, OR FISH.

AND EGGS. I HURLED EGGS YESTERDAY.

TOLD YOU HE WOULD.

HE WANTED TO TRY IT.

TRY IT IN **MY** ROOM. AND ROBOT PUKE IS FOUL.

WE SEEM TO KNOW A LOT ABOUT WHAT RALPH EATS.

HILO.

SO, WHO'S RALPH?

OF COURSE WE KNOW WHAT HILO EATS. HE EATS HERE MORE THAN D.J. DOES.

THAT'S NOT TRUE. I'M ALWAYS HERE WHEN HILO'S HERE.

WHOA! D.J.! I DIDN'T EVEN SEE YOU! YOU'VE BEEN SITTING HERE THE WHOLE TIME?

D.J.'S HERE?

44

45

HILO, YOU'VE **GOT** TO BE MORE CAREFUL AROUND LISA. SHE TOTALLY SUSPECTS THAT THERE'S SOMETHING DIFFERENT ABOUT YOU.

SHE'S RIGHT!

AND SHE LIKES YOU.

I LIKE HER.

NO, SHE **LIKE** LIKES YOU.

I KNOW. "**LIKE** LIKE." YOU GUYS HAVE SAID THAT BEFORE. I JUST DON'T UNDERSTAND WHY IT'S BAD TO LIKE SOMEBODY **TWICE**.

I **LIKE** LIKE YOU!

HEY, UNCLE TROUT!

HELLO THERE! HOW ARE YOU?

GOOD! YOU?

I'D LOVE TO! BUT I'VE GOT PILES TO DO HERE! AND I'M GETTING READY TO BARBECUE!

YOU REALLY NEED TO PROGRAM "UNCLE TROUT" TO SAY MORE IF YOU'RE GOING TO PRETEND HE'S YOUR GUARDIAN. PEOPLE ARE TOTALLY GOING TO THINK HE'S WEIRD.

WHIIIIIIIR.

TROUT'S FINE. PEOPLE ONLY SEE HIM THROUGH THE WINDOW. IT'S NOT ANY WEIRDER THAN HILO BUYING THIS HOUSE.

THE HOUSE WAS EASY! I JUST SOLD THE GOLD PARTS FROM THE BROKEN RANT ROBOTS AND PAID FOR THE HOUSE ON THE INTERNET. **AND** --

-- I GOT A TON OF MANGOES!

YOU LIKE MANGOES.

I **LIKE** LIKE MANGOES!

I'M JUST SAYING THAT IF YOU ATTRACT TOO MUCH ATTENTION, PEOPLE ARE GOING TO FIND OUT AND THEN CREEPY SCIENTISTS OR SECRET AGENTS WILL COME GET YOU.

REALLY?

OH YEAH. IT HAPPENS IN EVERY MOVIE ABOUT ALIENS COMING TO EARTH. WE --

WAIT. WHERE ARE WE GOING?

DOWNSTAIRS.

BEEP

SHUUUUP

49

CHAPTER

AND OUT WE GO

COBBLED IS A GREAT WORD, ISN'T IT? *ADJECTIVE*: ROUGHLY ASSEMBLE OR PUT TOGETHER SOMETHING FROM AVAILABLE ELEMENTS. YOU KNOW WHAT'S ANOTHER GREAT WORD? **MARMALADE.**

IT SMELLS REALLY NICE IN HERE.

MANGO.

AWESOME.

WHAT DO YOU NEED A LABORATORY FOR?

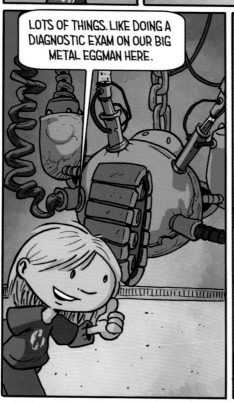

LOTS OF THINGS. LIKE DOING A DIAGNOSTIC EXAM ON OUR BIG METAL EGGMAN HERE.

BUT I'VE MOSTLY BEEN REPAIRING THE RANTS I DESTROYED.

THE RANTS! THEY WERE THE ROBOTS RAZORWARK SENT TO DESTROY EARTH!

I NEED ANSWERS, AND THEY PROBABLY HAVE THEM.

ANSWERS ABOUT WHAT?

ME.

AND **RAZORWARK.**

MY MEMORY IS FULL OF HOLES, AND THERE'S SO MUCH I DON'T REMEMBER ABOUT MY WORLD.

I NEED TO KNOW EVERYTHING ABOUT RAZORWARK IF I'M GOING TO BEAT HIM.

YOU DID BEAT HIM. RAZORWARK IS STUCK IN THAT VOID.

FOR NOW. BUT HE'S POWERFUL.

HE'LL GET OUT.

AND I HAVE TO STOP HIM.

IF I DON'T, HE'S GOING TO TAKE OVER MY WORLD.

AND HE WILL MAKE EVERY HUMAN BEING ON IT SUFFER.

I NEED TO REMEMBER.

I NEED TO UNDERSTAND WHO HE IS.

AND WHO I AM.

DIAGNOSTIC-IC. COMPLETED-TED. DOOP!

AAAH!

AAAH! LOVE THAT GREETING-TING!

WHAT IS THAT?!

OH, THAT'S **BEAMER.** HE'S THE ONLY RANT I COULD FIX ENOUGH TO GET HIS HIGHER BRAIN FUNCTION COOKING.

COOKING-ING!

DOOP

HOOOOONK

BUT THE BRAIN FUNCTION DOESN'T COOK **REAL** WELL.

Doop!

STILL, HE'S REMEMBERING MORE AND MORE. I BET YOU'LL BE ABLE TO TELL ME ALL KINDS OF STUFF ABOUT WHERE WE'RE FROM, WON'T YOU, BUDDY?

DoOooop

YEAH. TRYING TO FIND STUFF OUT IS **STILL** THE BEST PART OF NOT KNOWING SOMETHING.

D.J.?

YEAH?

THIS IS WHAT HILO NEEDS OUR HELP WITH.

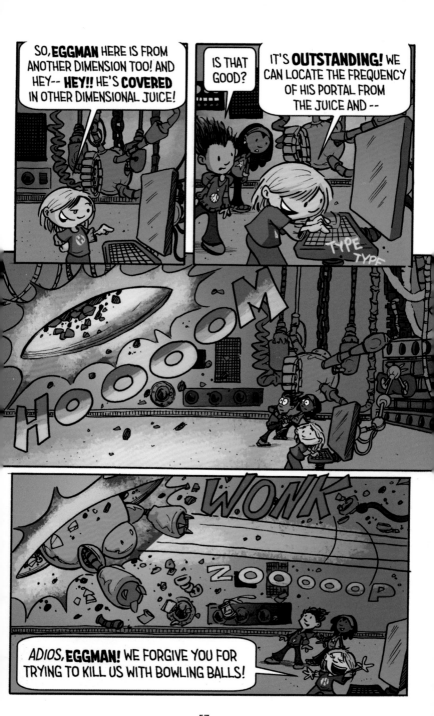

SO, YOU OPENED A PORTAL TO HIS WORLD?

YEAH! WE **WONKED** HIM HOME! THE JUICE HAS GOT **JUICE!** THAT WAS FUN. WE SHOULD DO THAT A LOT.

BING

WHOA. MAYBE WE WILL.

WHAT'S WRONG?

MORE PORTALS JUST OPENED ON THE OTHER SIDE OF TOWN, AND THERE'S **THINGS** COMING OUT OF THEM.

THIS COULD BE FUN.

FUN?!

KNOCK-KNOCK!

Doop

CHAPTER

5

POLLY

CLICK

THAT'S RIGHT, **WHALE BELLIES!** YOU'LL THINK TWICE BEFORE MESSING WITH --

TZOT

ZAAP

HOLY MACKEREL!

BIG HOLY MACKEREL!

VIKING HIPPOS AND A MAGICAL WARRIOR CAT. **OUTSTANDING.**

GREAT THANKS, TRAVELERS.

SHE **TALKS.**

YEAH.

SO OUTSTANDING.

I AM **POLLANDRA PACK WALLACE BRIMDALE KORIMAKO** OF THE MIGHTY **FURBACK CLAN.** APPRENTICE SORCERESS THIRD CLASS.

YOU MAY CALL ME **POLLY.**

I'M HILO. THIS IS D.J. AND GINA.

HEY.

HEY.

HILO, WHO FIRES BOLTS FROM HIS MITTS ...

MITTS?

I THINK SHE MEANS HANDS.

THEY'RE LASERS.

HILO LASER MITTS! YOU HAVE SAVED ME FROM GREAT PERIL! I AM IN YOUR DEBT UNTIL SUCH DEBT HAS BEEN PAID!

THAT'S COOL. BUT WE'RE JUST GOING TO SEND YOU AND THE MONSTER HIPPOS BACK TO YOUR WORLD.

OW.

THEY ARE **SLOBBERBACKS!** HURLING THIS VOMIT STINK FROM A DRAGON'S TONGUE **BACK** TO MY REALM IS JUST AND FAIR ...

I **DIG** THE WAY SHE TALKS.

YEAH. LIKE THOR.

OR SHERLOCK HOLMES.

BUT MESSIER.

YEAH.

BUT I AM A SORCERESS IN TRAINING BOUND BY MY HONOR. I **MUST** STAY IN YOUR CHARGE UNTIL MY DEBT HAS BEEN REPAID.

OKAY.

BUT THE MONSTER HIPPOS HAVE GOTTA GO BACK.

BEEP

HOOM

WONK

ZIIIIP

PROUD MAGIC, HILO LASER MITTS.

JUST WORKING THE PORTAL JUICE.

BATTLING BY YOUR SIDE WILL BE AN ADVENTURE!

YOU CAN SAY THAT AGAIN.

WHY WOULD I SAY THAT AGAIN?

HEY, LOOK...

THE **SNOW'S** GONE. THIS WHOLE FIELD... IT'S GONE ALL... **GRASSY.**

HA HA HA HA HA HA HA HA HA

HO! WHAT GREAT FUN!

YOU WANT TO HEAR SOMETHING **FUN?**

HILO'S HOUSE.

INTERRUPTING COW WH--

MOO!

HA HA HA HA HA HA HA HA

SO, THE COW **STOPS** YOU FROM TALKING! **HA HA HA HA!**

YEAH! YOU WANNA HEAR IT AGAIN?

INDEED!

I THINK WE NEED TO GET BACK TO POLLY TELLING US HOW SHE GOT TO EARTH.

THERE IS NOT MUCH TO TELL, GINA COOPER.

I WAS RUNNING OFF THE SLOBBERBACKS --

WHO HAD **STUPIDLY TRESPASSED ON FURBACK TERRITORY!**

WHEN A GATE OPENED AND WE WERE SWALLOWED UP.

MAY I HAVE MORE OF THIS DRINK?

IT'S **MILK.** DO YOU LIKE IT?

IT'S **DISGUSTING!** BUT I AM **FURBACK CLAN!** AND COMFORT IS FOR THE **WEAK!**

YOU SAID YOU WERE SWALLOWED BY **"A GATE"?**

AYE. GATES ARE COMMON IN MY REALM. GREAT DOORS THAT LEAD US INTO OTHER LANDS.

THIS GATE PULLED US INTO A VAST **NOTHINGNESS,** AND THEN WE WOUND UP HERE.

71

OH, AND LISA IS HERE.

HEY.

LISA?!

HOW MUCH DID YOU HEAR?

I HEARD THAT HILO'S A HIGHLY ADVANCED ANDROID FROM A FUTURISTIC DIMENSION, POLLY IS AN AWESOME MAGICAL-WORLD CAT WARRIOR, AND A VILLAIN NAMED RAZORWARK IS COMING TO EARTH.

THAT'S PRETTY MUCH EVERYTHING.

I JUST THOUGHT HILO WAS AN **ALIEN!** THIS IS **SO** MUCH COOLER!

DUDE!

OH, C'MON! THIS IS **OUTSTANDING!** WE'VE GOT A GANG HERE! A SQUAD, A TEAM --

A BAND.

A BAND! AND LISA'S RIGHT. WE'VE GOT TO SAVE THE WORLD.

FINE.

YOU DO **NOT** TELL ME WHAT TO DO.

OKAY.

SO, HILO... WHAT DO WE DO?

75

CHAPTER

THE BAND

79

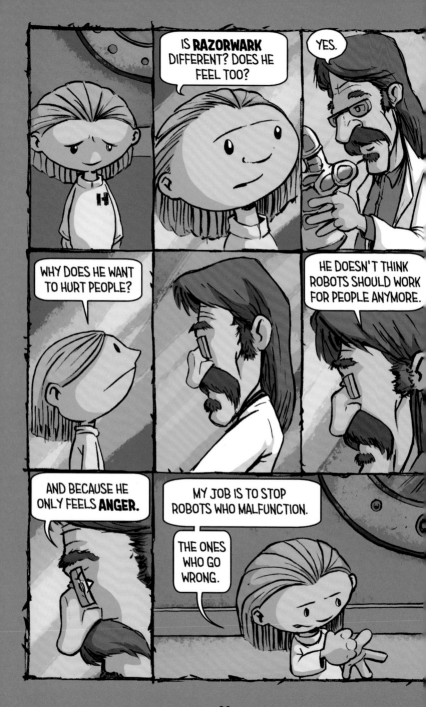

81

82

RAZORWARK WILL RAIN DOWN ON US ALL.

WHAT? WHAT DOES THAT MEAN?

THAT SOUNDS ... FAMILIAR. BEAMER, TELL ME ... WHAT IS THAT?

DOOP?

SHUUP

WHUP WUP WUP WUP

DING.

HELLO THERE! HOW ARE YOU?!

HEY, TROUT.

ZZZZZZ -- WHERE ARE YA?! I'LL TURN YOU INTO NEWTS! I'LL **NEWT** YA!

ZZZZZZ

SNORT

SHUP.

EAT HILO-LO-LO?

BEAMER ... PLEASE DON'T BRING ME FOOD. I'VE TOLD YOU. I CAN GET IT MYSELF.

WANT TO-TO-TO-WANT TO **HELP!**

PAT

DOOP ♪

I'D TELL A GROWN-UP IF I DIDN'T THINK THEY'D JUST FINK US OUT. HILO COULD BE DRAGGED OFF AND WIND UP BEING EXPERIMENTED ON IN A GOVERNMENT LAB.

HILO WOULD NEVER LET THEM DO THAT.

NO.

AND HE MIGHT BE FORCED TO HURT THEM.

D.J....

HE DOESN'T KNOW HOW POWERFUL HE IS.

YESTERDAY THAT EGGMAN ROBOT BLASTED THAT GIANT BALL OF ENERGY AT HIM....

IT FELT AS HOT AS THE **SUN**.

HILO JUST GRABBED IT... AND MADE IT **DISAPPEAR.**

I DON'T THINK HILO EVEN KNEW HE COULD **DO** THAT. HE'S DISCOVERING NEW STUFF ALL THE TIME.

BAD THINGS ARE COMING AFTER HIM.

BAD THINGS **HAPPEN** ALL AROUND HIM.

HE'S **DANGEROUS.**

HE DOESN'T MEAN TO BE... BUT HE IS.

YOU'RE **WRONG.** HE'D NEVER LET US GET HURT. HE'D NEVER LET **ANYONE** GET HURT....

I KNOW HE WOULDN'T MEAN TO...

BUT WHAT IF --

HE WON'T.

HILO'S HOUSE.

YOU'RE MAKING TRACKERS?

YEAH! THEY'LL BE ABLE TO INSTANTLY LOCATE WHERE A PORTAL OPENS.

BOOM!

YOU'RE GETTING REALLY GOOD AT MAKING STUFF.

YOU BET! I'M REMEMBERING ALL KINDS OF THINGS I CAN DO. LIKE MY **FREEZING ICE BREATH?** IT'S GETTING **BIGGER.**

HOOF!

IT LOOKS THE SAME.

NAH. IT'S **AT LEAST** TWO INCHES BIGGER. AND IT SMELLS LIKE **MANGO.**

THAT'S BECAUSE YOU JUST ATE SIX MANGOES.

91

EVERYTHING.

RAZORWARK IS TRYING TO TAKE OVER MY WORLD. MAYBE EARTH TOO. I'VE FORGOTTEN MOST OF MY LIFE.

I'M SCARED OF WHAT I MIGHT REMEMBER.

WHY?

THE MORE I REMEMBER, THE MORE I FEEL LIKE I'VE FORGOTTEN SOMETHING ... SOMETHING **TERRIBLE**.

BUT I KNOW IF ANYTHING BAD EVER HAPPENS, YOU'LL COME RUNNING TO HELP.

I WILL.

I KNOW.

THAT'S WHY I'M NOT SCARED.

WHAT THEY DON'T TELL YOU, MY ROBOT FRIEND **BEAMER**, IS THAT DRAGON EGGS ARE NOT **ONLY** HARD TO CRACK OPEN, BUT IF YOU EAT THEM, THEY GIVE YOU THE **WINDS** SOMETHING FIERCE.

WINDS!

DOOp

TELL ME AGAIN WHAT I AM EATING?

CORN NUTS.

munch munch

VILE. THEY ARE GOING TO MAKE ME RALPH. MAY I HAVE MORE?

WHO IS RALPH?

BING!

OH. WE'VE GOT OURSELVES A **BING.**

BING!

BING! BING! BING! BING! BING!

MANY BIG BINGS.

BINGO BANGO.

IT HAS BEGUN! **PORTALS** ARE OPENING **ALL** OVER TOWN.

THE TRACKERS LOCATE ANY PORTAL AND CAN FIND ANY **CREATURES** THAT POPPED OUT.

BUT MORE OUTSTANDING -- THEY'RE ALSO **PORTERS**! THEY CAN IDENTIFY THE PORTAL JUICE ON ANY CREATURE, OPEN A PORTAL BACK TO THEIR WORLD, AND **WONK** THEM BACK UP.

LIKE THIS GUY.

AAAAAAAH!

I GOT THIS.

BEEP

EASY PEASY.

WONK

HOOOM

BUT WAIT -- IF THERE ARE PORTALS EVERYWHERE AND MONSTERS RUNNING AROUND ALL OVER TOWN ... PEOPLE ARE GOING TO **SEE** IT.

AAAAAAAAH!

RAAAARGH!

BEEP

HOOM

WONK

MAYBE.

I'M RIGHT.

SO RIGHT.

HILO ...
PEOPLE ARE GOING TO
FIND OUT ABOUT YOU.
THAT'LL BE BAD.

THEY'LL TAKE
YOU AWAY.

NO. THEY
WON'T.

THEY WILL.

NO. I AM POLLANDRA
PACK WALLACE
BRIMDALE KORIMAKO.

I AM HONOR-BOUND TO
HILO LASER MITTS. **NO
ONE** WILL TAKE YOU. NOT
WHILE I HAVE BREATH IN
MY BODY AND FUR ON MY
BACK. YOU KNOW **WHY?**

HOW WILL YOU STOP PEOPLE FROM FINDING OUT ABOUT HILO?

I WON'T! BUT I WILL FIX IT!

NOW, THE TIME FOR TALK HAS ENDED!

WE HAVE WARGIES TO WONK BACK, A WORLD TO SAVE, AND THIS IS **THE BAND** TO DO IT!

HAZZAH!

HAZZAH!

CHAPTER 7

BING

103

OKAY, TIN MAN. I THINK YOU'VE MADE YOUR POINT.

DESTROY!

YES. I KNOW. YOU WANT TO DESTROY.

BUT THAT'S NOT YOUR FAULT. IT'S JUST HOW THEY MADE YOU.

THIS WON'T HURT. I'M JUST SHUTTING YOU OFF.

YOU'RE LUCKY, WARGIE!

LUCKY YOU GOT **WONKED!** OR I'D TURN YOUR **KEISTER** INSIDE OUT!

LUCKY.

LUCKY!

WHOA! I'VE GOT ANOTHER ONE THAT'S HOPPED OUT OF A PORTAL.

DEFEND YOURSELF, WARGIE!!

HANG ON, SOMETHING IS WEIRD ABOUT THIS ONE.

WEIRD **HOW,** GINA COOPER?!

WELL, THE SIGNAL SEEMS--

HOOO OOOAR

OOOOOAAAR

RIGHT. I'M GONNA BET AGAINST FRIENDLY.

I GOT THIS!

HUUUU UUUF

HOOOF

DANG IT. BUT IT'S TWO INCHES BIGGER, I'M SURE.

POOT

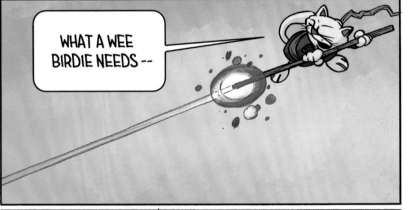

C'MON, C'MON! HOW HARD CAN IT BE TO FIND A SIGNAL ON AN ENORMOUS FIRE-BREATHING CHICKEN?!

BEEP.

YIKES. THAT'S AN ENORMOUS SIGNAL TOO. RIGHT AT...

D.J.'S HOUSE.

HILO!

D.J.'S HOUSE.

HOOOM

LOUIS, I THOUGHT YOU WERE TAKING ME TO BALLET ON YOUR WAY TO TENNIS.

WHUMP

I'M TAKING DEXTER TO PRACTICE.

HE JUST **CAME** FROM PRACTICE.

THAT WAS TRACK. NOW I'M GOING TO BAND PRACTICE.

PRACTICE IS **NOT** GOING TO HELP YOU GUYS.

MY BAND IS AWESOME. WE ROCK. WE ARE GOING TO BE **HUGE.**

THE ONLY WAY **YOUR** BAND IS GOING TO BE HUGE IS IF YOU **EAT** A LOT.

SNORT

MOOOOM!

JENNIFER, **I'LL** TAKE YOU TO BALLET. LOUIS, **PLEASE** TAKE DEXTER TO PRACTICE. AND, DEXTER, YOUR BAND **CERTAINLY** ROCKS.

116

WHO ROCKS?

DEXTER'S ROCK-AND-ROLL BAND.

MOM LIKES YOUR **ROCK-AND-ROLL** BAND.

SHUT UP.

YOU'RE HOME EARLY.

YES, THERE WAS A POWER OUTAGE AT THE OFFICE.

MOM!

REALLY? WHAT HAPPENED?

THEY COULDN'T FIND OUT. SO WE ALL --

MOM!!

JENNIFER! I'M COMING! YOU'RE **NOT** GOING TO BE LATE FOR --

HOLY MACKEREL.

CHAPTER 8

BRAVE BOY

ROOOOOOOOAAR!!

AAAAAAAAH!!

I'M GONNA BET AGAINST FRIENDLY!

AAAH!

SLAM

IT'S OKAY.
I GOT THIS.

BEEP

BLAM

BLAM

BEEP
BEEP
BEEP.

BLAM

IT'S NOT -- IT'S NOT WORKING!
THERE'S SUPPOSED TO BE
A PORTAL THAT --

BLAM

AAAAAAAAAAAAH!

BONK.

123

FOLLOW ME!

125

BUT WE DON'T HAVE A TREMENDOUS AMOUNT OF TIME TO EXPLAIN.

YOU DROPPED THE MONSTERS INTO THE EMPTY POOL?

YEP.

OUTSTANDING.

SEE? TROUBLE SHOWED UP AND **D.J. LIM** CAME **RUNNING**.

WE REALLY NEED TO DASH UP, BAND! MANY WARGIES TO WONK HOME!

YEP.

LET'S GO.

HANG ON!

MONSTERS ATE MY KITCHEN! THERE'S A TALKING **CAT!** AND HILO CAN **FLY!** I AM GOING TO NEED AN EXPLANATION!

NOW!

ONE EXPLANATION OF MONSTERS, TALKING CAT, AND FLYING HILO LATER ...

HILO'S A **ROBOT?**

THAT KIND OF EXPLAINS A LOT.

IT DOES?

WHO IS **BLAZERHAWK?**

RAZORWARK. HE'S THE BAD GUY.

130

THAT'S BEAUTIFUL! YEAH.

BLAAAP!

AND **THIS** IS THE VERY SNOT NAPPY MY OWN MUM GAVE **ME**!

YOU NEED A HONK?

I'M GOOD.

I LOVE THAT WOMAN!

BLAAAP

WE DISCOVERED THAT THE BIGGER THE CREATURE, THE LONGER IT TAKES TO LOCK ONTO A SIGNAL TO WONK THEM BACK.

BING

OH, **FEATHER HEAD** IS FINALLY READY.

YEP.

BEEP

HOOM...

BUCK?

WONK:

OUTSTANDING.

DOOP!

AAAH!

OH, HEY! THIS IS JUST BEAMER. HE'S DROPPING OFF MORE PORTERS. IF ANY CREATURES SHOW UP --

I'LL SHOW THEM. I'LL STAY HERE.

YEAH? YEAH.

SOMEBODY'S GOTTA LOOK AFTER OUR FAMILY.

AND THIS HILO BAND STUFF IS A **LITTLE** SCARIER THAN I THOUGHT.

BEAMER! HEAD HOME AND GET MORE PORTERS! WE NEED TO GIVE THEM OUT ALL OVER TOWN. WE'VE GOT TO KEEP CLOSING THE PORTALS SO RAZORWARK CAN'T COME THROUGH.

DOOP!

THANKS FOR THE HELP!

HELP!

WHOA.

HILO! WE'RE TRACKING A CREATURE OR SOMETHING!

BING

BINGO BANGO.

IT'S BIGGER THAN **ALL** OF THEM.

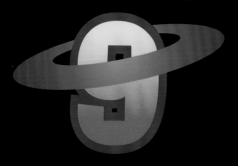

CHAPTER 9

VEGGIES

WHAT ARE THEY?

THEY ARE FROM **MY** WORLD. THEY ARE CALLED **RAPSCALLIONS.**

THEY ARE **VEGETABLES.**

137

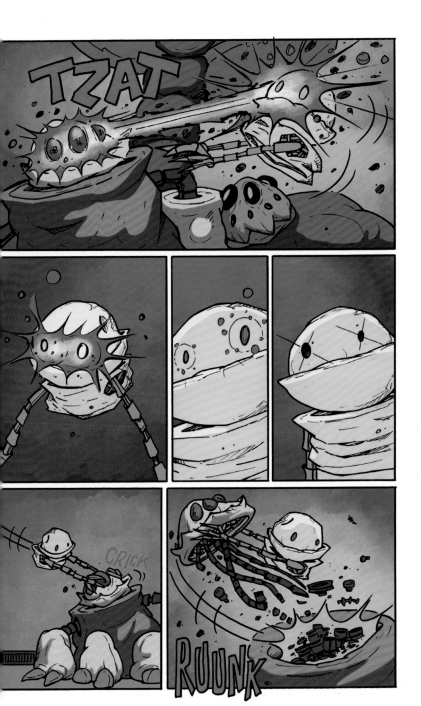

THE LAST RAPSCALLION WAS BANISHED FROM MY WORLD A THOUSAND YEARS AGO.

WE SENT IT INTO A GREAT EMPTINESS WHERE THEY COULD NEVER CAUSE HARM.

THE VOID.

THE PORTER CAN'T GET A FIX ON THE RAPSCALLIONS.

THERE'S TOO MANY OF THEM. AND THEY KEEP MAKING MORE. IT COULD TAKE **HOURS** TO GET A SIGNAL TO OPEN THE PORTAL BACK TO THE VOID.

IT COULD TAKE **DAYS**.

LOOK!

THEY'VE MADE IT TO TOWN!

THE **EARTH** WILL BE BURIED A **MILE DEEP.**

EVERY LIVING THING WILL DROWN IN THESE WEEDS.

WHAT DO WE DO?

WE PUSH BACK!

OH.

RIGHT BEHIND YA!
HAZZAH!

THIS IS
SO WRONG.

I REALLY LIKE MY VEGETABLES.

WHAT DO WE DO?

DO WHAT HILO DOES! KNOCK THEM BACK!

I CAN HELP WITH THAT!

TZOT

TZOT

BRE EEN.

149

SPLORG

BOOM

TOO MANY OF THEM! CAN'T BEAT THEM IF WE CAN'T STOP THEM FROM GROWING! I JUST --

GOOF

VICIOUS BRUSSELS SPROUTS!

TZOOT

150

GOOF

OH YEAH!

HWOOOSH

CREEAK

PROUD MAGIC.

YEAH.

GUYS! GUYS! GUYS! GUESS WHAT I FOUND OUT I COULD DO?!

YOU CAN FREEZE YOUR HANDS WITH YOUR BREATH AND BLAST ICE.

WELL, YEAH, BUT THAT WAS THREE MINUTES AGO. THIS IS **NEW**.

WHOOP!

SHUNK

BEEP

HOOM

OH MY.

POLLY!

THE PORTER OPENED HER PORTAL!

AND THERE'S ALSO DRIED APRICOTS IN THERE! WHICH ARE GROSS -- BUT I EAT 'EM!

BECAUSE YOU'RE FURBACK CLAN!

BECAUSE I AM FURBACK CLAN!

CHUNKA

HAZZAH!!

GREEEOK!

SPLOOSH

IT'S FREEING THE RAPSCALLIONS!

WHO IS THAT?!

NO.

CREEOK

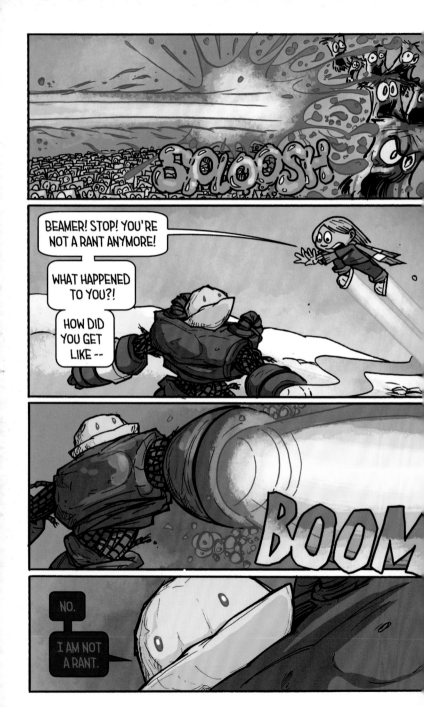

CHAPTER 10

BAD MACHINES

YOU'RE...
YOU'RE
HERE.

NOT EXACTLY.

I AM STILL
IN THE VOID.

I AM JUST
CONTROLLING
THIS LITTLE
ROBOT.

WHAT -- WHAT DID YOU DO TO BEAMER?

I COBBLED THIS BODY TOGETHER FROM THE PARTS OF THE OLD RANTS.

COBBLED.

IS THAT NOT A WONDERFUL WORD?

BEAMER ... HE'S STILL IN HERE. HE IS SIMPLY UNDER MY CONTROL.

I HAVE ALWAYS BEEN VERY GOOD AT CONTROLLING ROBOTS, HILO.

YOU WERE **NEVER** COMING TO EARTH. OPENING THE PORTALS, PRETENDING TO TRY TO WEAKEN THE WALLS BETWEEN THE VOID AND EARTH --

TZOT

BWEEN

IT WAS JUST SOMETHING TO KEEP **ME** BUSY WHILE THE **RAPSCALLIONS** GREW!

YES. I AM NOT COMING TO THIS WORLD YET.

I PLAN TO **CONQUER** IT FIRST.

THIS WORLD FALLS.

THEN OURS.

"RAZORWARK WILL RAIN DOWN ON US ALL."

AH.

YOU **DO** REMEMBER.

BOOM

172

BUT YOUR **HUMANS** WILL NOT.

D.J.!

I CAN'T HOLD ON!

I-- I'M **TRYING** -- I--

HILOOOOOOO!

LET ME GO!

SO YOU CAN SAVE YOUR HUMANS?!

NO!

WELL DONE ...
YOU'VE ... DESTROYED
ANOTHER ROBOT....

I **STOPPED**
YOU!

NO. I AM SAFELY IN THE VOID.
YOU HAVE JUST DESTROYED
YOUR LITTLE BEAMER.

NO.

YES.

NEVER FORGET WHAT
YOU'VE **BECOME**, HILO.

WHAT?

A BAD MACHINE.

GOOD-BYE, HILO.
I WILL SEE
YOU SOON ....

183

184

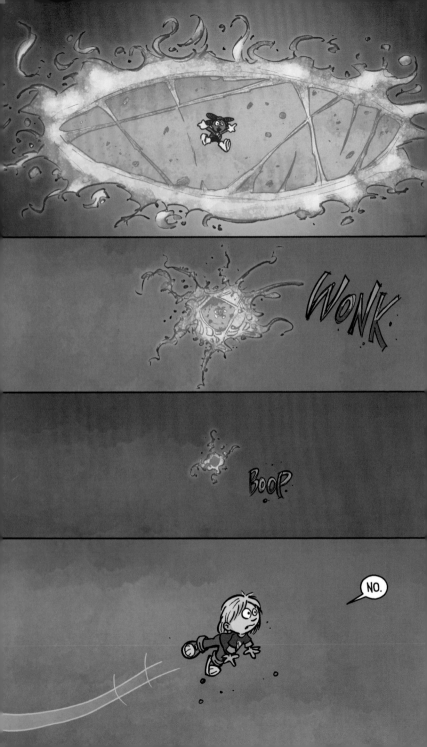

NO!

NO, NO, NO, NO.

OPEN THE PORTAL! **OPEN IT!**

WE HAVE TO GO GET HER!

I CAN'T.

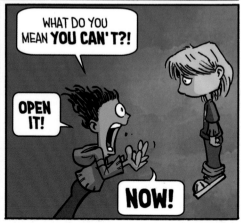

WHAT DO YOU MEAN **YOU CAN'T?!**

OPEN IT!

NOW!

I **CAN'T.**

THERE'S NO SIGNAL TO TRACK. THERE'S ... THERE'S NO WAY TO ...

ALL THE DOORS ARE CLOSED D.J.

I CAN'T OPEN IT.

NO.

NO.

GINA'S RIGHT. I AM DANGEROUS.

I REMEMBER NOW... I'VE DONE TERRIBLE THINGS.

THEN SOMETHING HAPPENED...

I CAN'T REMEMBER, BUT...

I BECAME **GOOD.**

I'LL GET GINA BACK.

I'LL GET HER BACK EVEN IF IT HURTS ME. EVEN IF I GET SO BROKEN THAT I CAN'T BE PUT BACK TOGETHER.

I'LL GET HER BACK.

WE'LL GET GINA.

I PROMISE.

I BELIEVE YOU.

BUT WE CAN'T GET HER RIGHT NOW.

WHY?

WELL, I THINK THE **ARMY** IS HERE TO TAKE ME AWAY.

END OF BOOK TWO

JUDD WINICK grew up on Long Island, where he spent countless hours doodling, reading **X-Men** comics and the newspaper strip **Bloom County**, and watching **Looney Tunes**. Today Judd lives in San Francisco with his wife, Pam Ling; their two kids; and their cat, Chaka. When Judd isn't collecting far more action figures and vinyl toys than a normal adult, he is a screenwriter and an award-winning cartoonist. Judd has scripted issues of bestselling comics series, including Batman, Green Lantern, Green Arrow, Justice League, and Star Wars. Judd also appeared as a cast member of MTV's **The Real World: San Francisco** and is the author of the highly acclaimed graphic novel **Pedro and Me**, about his **Real World** castmate and friend, AIDS activist Pedro Zamora. Visit Judd and Hilo online at **juddspillowfort.com.**